DAMIAN DROOTH
SUPERSLEUTH

THE CASE OF THE
POP STAR'S WEDDING

Other books by Barbara Mitchelhill

Eric and the Striped Horror
Eric and the Wishing Stone
Eric and the Pimple Potion
Eric and the Green-Eyed God
Eric and the Peculiar Pong
Eric and the Voice of Doom
Eric and the Old Fossil
Damian Drooth, Supersleuth:
The Case of the Disappearing Daughter
Damian Drooth, Supersleuth:
How to be a Detective
The Great Blackpool Sneezing Attack
Kids on the Run

DAMIAN DROOTH SUPERSLEUTH

THE CASE OF THE POP STAR'S WEDDING

BARBARA MITCHELHILL

Illustrated by TONY ROSS

Andersen Press • London

For Tom who likes football
and Alexandra who loves pink (B.M.)

First published in 2002 by
Andersen Press Limited,
20 Vauxhall Bridge Road, London SW1V 2SA
www.andersenpress.co.uk

Reprinted 2005, 2006, 2007

British Library Cataloguing in Publication Data
available

ISBN 978 1 84270 561 2

Phototypeset by Intype London Ltd
Printed in the UK by CPI Bookmarque, Croydon, CR0 4TD

Chapter 1

My name is Drooth. Damian Drooth.
Crime buster extraordinary. Ace
detective.

Let me tell you about my latest case.

It started when a letter arrived for
Mum. It was addressed to Mrs
Drooth, Home Cooking Unlimited.

'Guess who this is from!' she
shrieked. I could tell she was in a real
tizz.

So I read the letter.

Dear Mrs Drooth,
I was wondering if you would be
interested in providing the food for my
wedding. Perhaps you could come to see
me and discuss the menu.
                    Yours sincerely,
                    Tiger Lilly

I stared at the signature. I was
gobsmacked.
    '**Tiger Lilly?**' I yelled. (It was
difficult to stay calm.) '**The singer?**
One of the Bay Babes?'
    Mum nodded and my head
exploded. She was my most favourite
singer EVER! I was her NUMERO
UNO fan! Wow! Wow! Wow!
    That morning, Mum telephoned
Tiger Lilly and arranged a meeting.
    'I'll come with you,' I said.
    'I don't think so,' said Mum as she
wrote the date in her diary.

'You might get lost,' I insisted.

'I can read a map, Damian.'

'I could be your secretary and take notes.'

'I don't want a secretary.'

I tried a different approach.

'Right! I'll go on hunger strike if you don't take me!'

Mum sighed. 'Don't be stupid, Damian!' she said. 'NO!'

In the end, she gave in. My mum's brain power is no match for my razor-sharp cunning.

And so I got to meet the fabulous Tiger Lilly.

Chapter 2

Tiger Lilly's place was mega huge! Even the drive was longer than our street. As we pulled up outside the front door, there she was waiting for us on the steps. A Star! Some guys would have gone wild. But not me! Fame doesn't bother me. Even though her eyes were deep blue and her hair was blonde and right down to her waist – I stayed cool.

Then Mum spoke.

'This is my little boy, Damian,' she said in her mumsy voice. 'I hope you don't mind him coming with me. There was no one to look after him – and he's inclined to get into trouble.'

I ask you! Embarrassing or what? But I stuffed my hands in my pockets and just said, 'Hi!' as if I met celebrities every day.

We followed Tiger Lilly down the hall and into a fantastic room with big comfy chairs and a dangly chandelier.

'Well, Damian,' she said, as she poured us some tea. 'I've got a little brother and he's always in trouble, too!'

'It may seem like trouble to some,' I said, darkly. 'But the fact is I work undercover. I'm a Private Eye.'

I could see she was dead impressed.

'I track down crooks . . . bank robbers . . . forgers . . . that kind of thing.'

Tiger Lilly turned and looked at Mum.

'You didn't tell me you'd got your own detective agency, Mrs Drooth!' she said. Then she winked – or maybe she had something in her eye. 'He'll be useful on the day of the wedding. Don't want any of my presents getting stolen, eh?'

Mum looked horrified. 'Oh Damian won't be here on your wedding day,' she said. 'I wouldn't want him here with all your guests around. He'll just get in the way.'

Cheek! After all the times I've helped out! Only a few breakages. Only a few mistakes. That's understandable, isn't it?

Luckily, Tiger Lilly *insisted* I went. 'You organise the food, Mrs Drooth, and Damian can keep a lookout for suspicious characters.'

Mum couldn't say anything, could she? I had been employed as a private detective at the Wedding-of-the-Year.

Chapter 3

There were three weeks to go before
the wedding and I had to be on top
form. I needed to sharpen up my
sleuthing skills. In my Supersleuth
Notebook, I had a theory of detection
to help me in my work:
ANYONE WITH EYES SET CLOSE
TOGETHER IS NOT TO BE
TRUSTED.

(This was very useful in my first case – known for miles around as the case of the Disappearing Daughter.)

But one theory wasn't enough. After all, I could be up against hardened criminals at the wedding. I decided to spend the time studying detective stories. There were some great ones in my comics. Mum didn't understand, of course.

'Why not read a proper book?' she said. But I stuck to it regardless.

After ten days of serious study, I came up with:

ANYONE WITH A BEARD (PARTICULARLY A DARK ONE) IS PROBABLY UP TO NO GOOD.

Working out a theory is one thing. Proving it is another. This is how I did it. *(For those who want to pick up hints about detective work, I've copied out my notebook in my best handwriting.)*

MUNDAY

Our teecher, Mr Grimethorpe is off sick. They say it's stress. But how can that be? Teechers have it dead eesy! If you ask me, he spends too much time showting and thumping his desk.

Our new teecher is mr Symes <u>WHO HAS A BEARD</u>.

<u>TUSDAY</u>
mr Symes is ded keen on muny.
He counts dinner muny twice.
He needz watching.

<u>WENSDAY</u>
9.15 MS counts trip
muny 3 times!!!!!!
9.30 MS puts muny in
his breefcase.
THIS PROVES HE IS A
THEEF.

9.35 Work out cunning plan in back of maths book.

9.45 Put plan into acshun. Stuff breefcase under my jumper. Creep out of classroom when MS isn't looking. Go to find Mrs Frank our skool seckreetary.

10.0 Skool office locked. No sine of Mrs Frank. Probably making tea and choclut biskits for the Head.

10.10 Hide breefcase in clokeroom. Will pick it up later.

10.15 Go back to class.

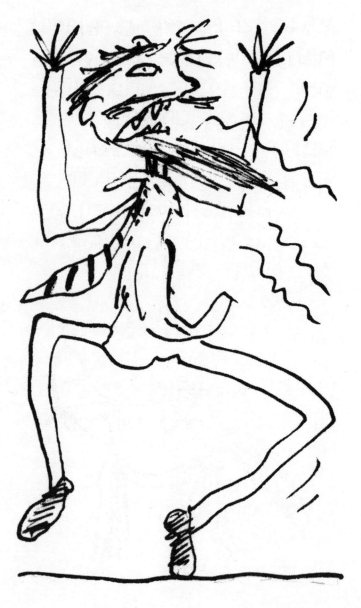

MS has a temper as bad as Mr Grimethorpe. He makes me stay in at brake and write lines. FOR NO REASON. He is a reel criminal for shoor.

11.0 Police arrive. How do they know about the muny? MS looks ded wurrid. No wunder!

21

THERSDAY

9.0 No sine of Mr Symes. I expect he's in prison.

I will not menshun my part in his downfall to the police.

So my Theory of the Beard was proved. Now I could track down the craftiest criminal who dared to go to Tiger Lilly's wedding.

Chapter 4

On the morning of the wedding, Mum
was in a real flap. Me? I'd got my gear
together, my notepad and my pen –
and I was ready to take on the big
names of the underworld, if necessary.

'Damian!' Mum shouted. 'Don't
stand there in a daze. Help me get
these puddings into the van.'

I ask you! Does James Bond carry puddings for his mum? No! But that day, she was in a bit of a mood. So I did it. I picked up a big chocolate mousse and carried it as carefully as I could. Was it my fault if the path was uneven? Was it my fault if I slipped?

Mum didn't speak to me all the way to Tiger Lilly's place. She just gripped the wheel and frowned at the road ahead. She was in a real mood.

When we reached the house, there was a security man on the gate. He was huge and wore a badge with DEAN on it. I must say, I was surprised that Tiger Lilly had employed him when she knew I was coming.

Mum stopped and wound down the window.

'Catering,' she said.

'I need to see your passes,' said Dean.

Mum handed her card out of the window. I leaned over and flashed the detective badge I had made the night before. We were waved straight in. No problem.

The lawn in front of Tiger Lilly's
house was filled with an enormous tent
(called a *marquee*). And there were
loads of people milling around,
carrying chairs and arranging flowers.
Mum parked the van behind the
marquee and started unloading the

food. She was dashing backwards and
forwards like a wild thing carrying
trays and dishes and got really out of
breath. If you ask me, she's not at all
fit. She could do with a good work-out
at the gym.

I offered to help but she wasn't

keen. She said she'd rather do it
herself.

'All right,' I said. 'I'll go and look
round the grounds for crooks and
that.'

Mum gave me one of her looks. 'You
dare get into trouble!' she shouted over
a pile of vol-au-vents. 'I've got enough
to think about without worrying about
you.'

'Stay cool!' I said. 'I'm in control.'

Mum's face turned scarlet. Probably
her blood pressure. It's best to ignore
it. So I put on my shades and walked
away.

It wasn't long before I saw a man who was dead suspicious. He was wearing a black suit with a white shirt and was carrying a black leather case.

Spooky! And – guess what? His eyes were really close together. (Detection Theory number 1.) If that wasn't enough – he had a BLACK BEARD, too! (Detection Theory number 2.) I had hit the jackpot! This man was a mega criminal.

I did a quick sketch and made some notes in my Supersleuth Notebook. Then I followed him into the house. It was obvious he was planning to steal the wedding presents.

Chapter 5

I walked behind him with my back pressed against the wall. Just like detectives on TV. But, before I got close, somebody shouted, 'Hey, kid!' and a security guard grabbed me by the collar.

'What do you think you're doing in here, eh?'

I checked his badge (which said CURT) and showed him mine.

'I'm with Mum's catering company,' I said.

Curt grunted.

'I'm Tiger Lilly's personal protection officer.'

Curt laughed! What was so funny?

'Out you go, sonny,' he said, as if I was a kid. 'Go and find your mum.'

Of course, I did no such thing. I owed it to Tiger Lilly to watch over her presents. I walked away, pretending to head for the marquee. When I was sure that Curt had gone, I hurried back towards the house and sneaked down the side.

As I peeped in through a window, I saw the presents spread out on a table. Each one had a label showing who had sent it. There were masses of silver plates and goblets – stuff like that. There were old paintings, too, that must have been worth a bomb. But in the middle of it all was a fantastic diamond necklace. A large label said, 'To Tiger Lilly on our wedding day from Gary with love and kisses.' YUK!

Tiger Lilly was marrying Gary Blaze. I didn't know why. He was a football player with skinny legs and no hair. He was useless at everything except scoring goals. Why did Tiger Lilly fall for someone like that, I ask you? She needed a guy with laser brainpower. Someone who could spot a thug a mile away.

As I looked through the window, the man with the beard walked into the room. He stood and stared at the diamond necklace. It was obvious that he was going to nick it when the not-very-bright security guard (CURT) wasn't looking.

I worked out a plan. I ran round to the front door, hid behind the ivy and waited. Ten minutes later the man in black came out and I followed him down the path. Half way, he stopped, looked at his watch and started running towards the marquee. Suspicious or what? But I was onto him.

By that time, the reception was in full swing. The crook went round the back of the tent, lifted a loose flap and sneaked in. He was cunning all right! But he wasn't going to get away.

I hurried to the main entrance of the tent. Inside, everybody was eating and talking. I could see Tiger Lilly looking fantastic in a long white dress with flowers in her hair and silver nail varnish. Gary Blaze looked stupid in a blue suit. (What did she see in him?)

I looked round trying to spot the
thief. YES! There he was. Hiding
amongst the band. Pretending to play
a saxophone. Very clever, I don't
think.

If he thought he would get away
with the necklace – he was making a
big mistake!

Chapter 6

I had to tell Tiger Lilly what was going
on. I knew she'd be dead impressed
when she heard I'd saved her diamond
necklace. I started running towards her
but, before I could get near, a hand
landed on my shoulder and a security
guard (KELVIN) pulled me up sharp.

I yelled. But nobody came to help.
They were too busy stuffing
themselves with Mum's food (chicken
and all the trimmings).

'What do you think you're playing
at?' said Kelvin as he dragged me
outside.

I started to explain. 'I'm tracking down . . .'

But before I could finish, Curt came dashing out of the big house shouting, 'Come quick, Kelvin! Quick!'

Kelvin dropped me like a hot potato and ran. I followed, of course.

Something was up!

'The diamond necklace has been nicked,' said Curt.

'I know that,' I said – just to be helpful.

The guards turned and looked at me.

'How do you know?' said Kelvin.

'I'm a Private Eye,' I said, holding out my badge.

They raised their eyebrows and smirked. But I ignored them.

'I was watching the presents when I saw someone take the necklace.'

(It was *nearly* true. I *almost* saw him. It couldn't have been anyone else, could it?)

I flicked open my Supersleuth Notebook.

'The thief was a tall, thin male with a beard, wearing a black suit, a white shirt and carrying a black case.'

They looked at me as if I'd crawled out from under a stone.

'Stupid boy!' said Curt. 'That's Dave. He plays in the band!'

I smiled, knowingly. 'Just a cover for his criminal activities,' I said. 'I reckon the necklace is in the case.'

They snorted and pushed me to one side.

'Ring the police, Curt,' said Kelvin. 'Don't tell any of the guests or the wedding will be ruined.'

Curt got out his mobile and dialled 999.

'As for you!' said Kelvin, turning to me. 'I thought we'd sent you back to your mother.'

He didn't let me explain. He slung me over his shoulders like a sack of carrots. Cheek!

I thought he'd take me to the
refreshment tent. But he didn't. He
took me to the van.

'Right!' he said, swinging open the
back door. 'You can stay there until
your mum's finished with the food.
Then *she* can look after you.' He flung
me inside and slammed the door shut.

I didn't have the energy to try to escape. Suddenly I felt weak. My blood sugar was dropping. My brain was slowing down. I knew it was the stress of chasing criminals – and lack of food. Luckily, I had spotted a chocolate gateau in the back of the van. It's one of my favourites. So I had a slice, in the interest of successful crime detection.

(REMEMBER THIS TIP: Chocolate gateau is excellent for energy.)

I felt so much better after one slice that I had another. The more I ate, the more my brainpower increased. It was amazing! Of course, I hid the plate so Mum wouldn't notice the missing gateau. I didn't want her getting upset.

Now I was ready for action.
Escaping would be no problem. The
lock on the van door was broken, see.
When Mum locked it up at night, she
had to put a chain round the handles.
She said it was cheaper than having a
new lock fitted. But the guard didn't
know that, did he? He thought he'd
locked me in. Tee hee!

Slowly, I opened the door and
peeped out. I was a few metres from
the entrance of the marquee. I could

see Tiger Lilly (still looking gorgeous) and the band on the far side. But there were security guards everywhere. It was almost impossible to get in without being seen. So how could I reach the thief and save the diamond necklace?

Chapter 7

Being a trained detective, I soon had
the problem sorted.

Between the van and the entrance
was a large trolley with the wedding
cake on top. Perfect! All I had to do
was distract the waiter who was
standing nearby. (He was wrinkled and
stooping – at least forty.) Then I would
hide under the trolley.

'Excuse me!' I said, climbing out of the van. 'Somebody's looking for you. I can hear them shouting over there.'

The waiter looked puzzled but went
off round the back of the van. That
was my chance. I dashed across, lifted
the cloth and slipped onto the bottom
layer of the trolley.

The waiter was back in no time.

'Huh! Young 'uns,' I heard him
mutter. 'Up to their tricks!'

Then he pushed the trolley into the
marquee, across the wooden floor and
stopped in front of the bride's table.
Everybody cheered and clapped as
Tiger Lilly and the bald footballer
walked towards it to cut the cake.

That's when I leapt out.

'HOLD EVERYTHING!' I shouted.
(I had heard a detective say this in a
film. I thought it sounded good.)

'STAND CLEAR!' I added, just for
good measure. 'THERE IS A CROOK
IN HERE AND HE'S STOLEN A
DIAMOND NECKLACE!'

I must admit, I was surprised Tiger Lilly didn't rush to my side. Hadn't she understood what I'd said?

Instead, security guards were running towards me from every corner of the tent like crazy gorillas.

I jumped back onto the trolley and, pushing off with one foot, I skimmed over the floor towards the band.

'IT'S HIM!' I shouted. 'THE ONE WITH THE SAXOPHONE! HE STOLE THE NECKLACE AND IT'S IN HIS BLACK CASE!'

At this point, the trolley ran out of control and smashed into the band. I whizzed through the air like Superman and landed on the stage while the cake shot across the floor leaving behind a lake of white icing and cream.

I stared up into the face of the crook. (His beard looked even worse close up.)

'GOTCHA!' I said.

But it was the man *behind* him who suddenly leapt off the stage and made a run for it. Unluckily for him, he skidded on the splodge of cream. His feet flew out from under him and he crashed onto his back like a beached whale.

Meanwhile, I clambered across the stage and reached in his case.

'I think he's forgotten something,' I called out and held up the necklace for all to see. Now everybody was on their feet. They stood in a great circle round the crook, pushing and shoving to get a better look.

All this excitement – and then the police arrived.

'What's going on?' said the Inspector. 'Have you caught the thief?'

'Thanks to this boy, we have,' said Tiger Lilly. 'This is Damian Drooth and he could teach the police a thing or two about solving crimes.'

As she spoke, she put her arm round my shoulder. I almost fainted with pride.

Chapter 8

I expect you're wondering how I managed to track down the jewel thief. After all, he didn't have a beard like my first suspect.

Well, I must admit there was a bit of a mistake. You see, I'm not brilliant at names of instruments and stuff. So when I shouted, 'It's the one with the saxophone!' I got it wrong. I should have said a trumpet.

For your information, this is a trumpet . . .

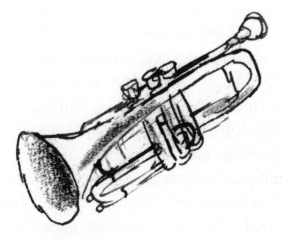

this is a saxophone.

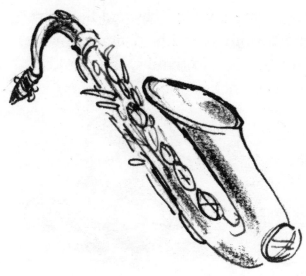

But it didn't matter. As it turned out, the man who stole the necklace *really was* playing the saxophone. Lucky mistake, eh?

As for Tiger Lilly, she was thrilled I'd foiled the crook. I asked her if she'd sign my CDs and she said, 'Oh Damian, I'll give you a copy of every CD I've ever made **and** sign it for you.' Then she kissed me on the cheek. That was a bit girlie for me but it was OK, really.

Gary Blaze went all smarmy and said, 'Thanks ever so much, Damian.' I think he's a wimp. He said he'd give me a football and he'd sign it for me. But I said, 'No thanks. I'm not keen on football.'

Everybody cheered me and they
made a great fuss. They asked me what
I would like to eat and made me sit at
one of the posh tables.

'Sorry, Damian,' said Kelvin when
he brought me two plates of food.
'We've run out of chocolate gateau.
Will strawberries do?'

It's the thought that counts.

When everything had calmed down and most of the police had gone, Inspector Crockitt came over to talk to me. I'd met him before. He tries to pick up tips on solving crimes.

'How did you catch him, Damian?' he asked.

I'm too modest to tell a police inspector how to do his job. But I like to help.

'I've got this theory about beards,' I said.

'Is that how you solved this case?' he asked.

I could see he was keen to know. 'Maybe,' I said, winking at him. 'But maybe I got lucky.'

They don't call me Supersleuth for nothing.